Strangers on a Train

'Guy, I just thought. Oh, yes! You murder my father and I'll murder Miriam. The police will never find us. We're strangers, we met on a train and nobody knows we're friends. It's perfect.'

After Guy Haines meets Charley Bruno on a train he tries to forget about Bruno's plan for murder. But from this moment Guy is pulled deeper and deeper into a world of madness, lies and death. Two murders follow one after the other – there is no escape.

Patricia Highsmith was born in America in 1921 and now lives in Switzerland. She decided to become a writer when she was sixteen, and *Strangers on a Train* was her first novel. It appeared in 1950 and is still her best-known book.

Patricia Highsmith is one of the best crime writers of this century and has written more than 20 books and short stories. She writes about her own special world of fear and anger and murder, and it is often difficult to know who is good and who is bad in her books. Her most famous character is a murderer called Ripley.

Alfred Hitchcock made a film of *Strangers on a Train* in 1951, but he changed the story. In the film Guy Haines is a famous tennis-player and not an architect; his girlfriend, Anne, has a younger sister who helps Guy, and Bruno's mother is an old lady who paints bad pictures. This film has a happy ending for Guy, too, but it is still a very good film and exciting to watch.

Strangers on a Train

PATRICIA HIGHSMITH

Level 4

Retold by Michael Nation
Series Editors: Andy Hopkins and Jocelyn Potter

Addison Wesley Longman Limited
Edinburgh Gate, Harlow,
Essex CM20 2JE, England
and Associated Companies throughout the world.

ISBN 0 582 40254 9

Strangers on a Train copyright 1950 by Patricia Highsmith
This adaptation first published by Penguin Books 1995
This edition first published 1998

Text copyright © Michael Nation 1995
Illustrations copyright © Ian Andrew 1995
All rights reserved

The moral right of the adapter and of the illustrator has been asserted

Typeset by Datix International Limited, Bungay, Suffolk
Set in 11/13pt Lasercomp Bembo
Printed in Spain by Mateu Cromo, S.A. Pinto (Madrid)

Published by Addison Wesley Longman Limited in association with
Penguin Books Ltd., both companies being subsidiaries of Pearson Plc

Dictionary words:

- As you read this book, you will find that some words are in darker black ink than the others on the page. Look them up in your dictionary, if you do not already know them, or try to guess the meaning of the words first, and then look them up later, to check.

CHAPTER ONE

The train rushed along angrily. Guy was thinking about Miriam. He saw her round pink face, her cruel mouth . . . he started to hate her.

'Perhaps Miriam doesn't want a **divorce**,' Guy thought unhappily. 'But she's **pregnant** and it's not my child, and she must want to marry the father. Why does she want to see me, though? She can get a divorce without that. Perhaps she doesn't want a divorce, only money.'

Miriam sometimes asked him for money and he always sent it because she was good at making trouble and Guy didn't want his mother to be unhappy. In Metcalf, Guy's home town, Miriam pretended that Guy lived in New York so he could succeed as an **architect** before he sent for her.

Guy thought about his girlfriend Anne and how much he loved her, and about the important job he had in Florida. He felt happy. 'Soon . . .' Guy said to himself. 'Soon . . .' He started to read his book.

After he had read half a page Guy looked up and saw a young man sitting opposite him. The young man was very tall and thin, and he smiled shyly at Guy as if he did not know whether to speak or not. Guy moved in his seat and accidentally touched the young man's foot.

'Sorry,' Guy said.

'That's all right,' the man said. 'Say, where are we? Do you know?'

'Texas.'

The young man took a small bottle of whisky from his pocket and offered it to Guy with a friendly smile. He had a very large head, his face did not look stupid or intelligent, or

1

young or old. His eyes were red and tired, but his skin was as smooth as a girl's.

'No, thanks,' Guy said.

The young man drank some of the whisky, then he asked, very politely, 'Where are you going?'

'Metcalf.' Guy wanted to read his book.

'Nice town, Metcalf,' the young man said. 'Are you going on business?'

'Er, yes.' Guy turned the page of his book.

'What business?' the young man asked, like a child.

'I'm an architect.'

'That's interesting,' he said. He put his hand forward. 'My name's Bruno, Charles Anthony Bruno.'

Guy shook his hand. 'Guy Haines,' he said.

'Do you live in New York, Guy?' Bruno asked.

'Yes I do.'

'I live on Long Island,' Bruno said. 'I'm going to Santa Fe on holiday.'

Guy wanted to read, or to think, but he could feel this man who wanted to talk all the time looking at him. The train stopped and Guy took a walk outside for some fresh air, but it wasn't fresh, it was hot and thick. He went back to the train for some dinner.

'Hello!' Bruno sat down at Guy's table. 'Look, I've got a private room. Have dinner with me, that'll be nice.'

'No, thanks. I . . .' Guy said.

'Yes!' Bruno said. He stood up quickly. He seemed drunk. He ordered dinner for two in his private room, then he walked away, stepping carefully.

Guy followed him. 'Why not?' he thought. 'He's someone to talk to.'

Bruno's room was very untidy. There were clothes, magazines, cigarettes, chocolates everywhere on the floor and the seats. In the middle of the floor Guy saw four big bottles of whisky in a straight line. A waiter brought dinner and they started to eat, and to drink the whisky.

'What are you going to build in Metcalf, Guy?' Bruno asked, his mouth full of food.

'Nothing,' Guy said. 'My mother lives in Metcalf, it's my home.'

Bruno stopped eating. 'Do you like your mother, Guy?'

'Yes.'

'Your father, too?'

'He's dead,' Guy said.

'Oh. Yeah, I like my mother, too,' Bruno said. 'She's coming to Santa Fe. We do everything together.' Bruno stopped suddenly. 'Do you think that's strange?'

'No,' Guy said.

'Mother gives me money,' Bruno said. He lit a cigarette and drank more whisky. 'Father never gives me anything. He's rich, too!' Bruno shouted. 'I want my own money!'

Then Bruno laughed. 'Father would like you, Guy. You're good and quiet, and you've got a good job, too. Me? I don't want to work. Why should I? I don't feel like it.' Bruno laughed again. 'Father wants me to go into his business. Like Hell I will!' Bruno pushed his cigarette into the dish of butter next to his plate. 'He never gives me money – I know he doesn't like me. I don't like him. You know, Guy, sometimes, I could kill him.'

Bruno looked at Guy. 'Did you ever want to murder someone, Guy?'

Guy wasn't listening, he was thinking about Anne and Miriam and Florida. It was all mixed up in his head.

'Tell me about you, Guy,' Bruno asked. 'What kind of things do you build?'

'What?' Guy tried to think. 'Oh, houses, offices . . .'

'Are you married, Guy?'

'No. Yes. Er, well, I'm separated. I left three years ago,' Guy said. He didn't want to tell Bruno these things.

'Oh? Why is that, Guy?'

'I think we were too young . . .'

'Do you love her?' Bruno's eyes weren't tired now. They were bright and looked straight at Guy. 'You take love seriously, don't you, Guy?'

Guy didn't answer this.

'What kind of girl is your wife?' Bruno asked.

'She's pretty, red hair, a little fat,' Guy said. 'We're going to get a divorce,' he said.

'Why? Why now? Why not before?' Bruno's eyes were very bright.

'She's pregnant,' Guy said. He didn't like saying it.

'Oh, boy!' Bruno said. 'I hate women like that, don't you?'

'Well, no . . . I,' Guy said. 'It happens.'

Bruno pulled the cigarette in and out of the butter. 'Men go to women like her like flies go to rubbish,' he said. 'What's her name?'

'Miriam, Miriam Joyce.' Guy tried to change the subject. 'Well, Bruno,' he said. 'If you don't want to work, what do you want to do?'

'I think a man needs to try everything once. You know, everything – travel, and women, and, uh, robbery . . . and murder.' He stopped and looked at Guy with a worried face. 'Did you ever want to kill someone, Guy?'

'No.' Guy was starting to feel drunk.

Bruno picked up another bottle of whisky and tried to open it. 'You know, Guy, the police don't catch most murderers.' He was very drunk and the top of the bottle flew off. Whisky went all over the floor.

'Really?' Guy said.

'You know, Guy, the police don't catch most murderers.' He was very
drunk and the top of the bottle flew off.

'No, they don't.' Bruno drank from the bottle. 'Come to Santa Fe with me, Guy! I like you!'

'I can't,' Guy said 'After Metcalf, I have to go to Florida. I'm going to build a sports club there.'

'Oh, Guy!' Bruno looked at him the way a little boy looks at his father. 'That's great. You must be very good.'

Guy smiled, 'Well, thanks . . .'

'But,' Bruno said, 'if Miriam makes trouble now – about the divorce – if she came to Florida, Guy, well, you could lose the job, couldn't you?'

Guy thought, 'That's the kind of thing Miriam would do.'

'You could murder her for that, couldn't you, Guy?'

'No,' he said.

'I could make a plan for murdering your wife, Guy,' Bruno said. 'You might want to use it some time.'

'No!'

'Oh, Guy!' Bruno stood up suddenly and waved the bottle about. 'Oh!' he shouted. 'Guy! I just thought. Oh, yes! You murder my father and I'll murder Miriam. The police will never find us. We're strangers, we met on a train and nobody knows we're friends. It's perfect.'

Now the room was a little Hell. It was very hot, Bruno's face was red and his mouth was wide open, shouting, shouting.

'No, no!' Guy said. He ran out of the room, then he opened one of the windows and breathed in the cold night air.

'Guy?' Bruno stood behind him and put his hand on Guy's back. 'I'm sorry.' Guy pulled away from him. 'Oh, please, Guy.' He was like a dog.

'It's all right,' Guy said. 'Let's forget it.'

'OK, thanks.' Bruno smiled. 'Do you want another drink?'

'No, I'm going to bed,' Guy said.

Before he went to sleep Guy remembered that his book was

still in Bruno's room. He didn't go back for it. He never wanted to see Bruno again.

CHAPTER TWO

When he got to Metcalf Guy phoned Miriam and they met outside their old school. It was a hot day and Miriam wore a big white hat. Her face looked fatter than Guy remembered and there were little lines under her eyes.

'Hello, Guy,' Miriam said and smiled, but shut her little mouth quickly to hide her bad front teeth. She looked soft and sticky.

'Hello, Miriam,' he said. 'How are you? When will the child come?'

'January,' she said.

'She's two months' pregnant,' Guy thought. He said, 'You must want to marry him . . . the man?'

'You see,' she said, 'it's a bit difficult.'

'Difficult?'

'He's married, Guy.' Miriam was looking in front of her, speaking as if he wasn't there.

'But we can still get divorced,' he said.

'Owen can't get divorced until September, that's four months,' Miriam told him.

'We could get divorced now,' Guy said.

'Could we wait?' she asked. 'I think I'd like to go away for a few months.'

'What do you mean?'

'Your mother told me about your job in Florida,' Miriam said with her little smile. She looked up at Guy with her dead eyes. 'I want to come with you, and stay until December.'

'No,' he said. 'You can't do that.'

He tried to talk to her. 'Is there anything we can do about this, Miriam?' he asked.

'If you don't take me with you, I'll come alone,' she said.

'Then I won't take the job.'

'You won't do that,' she said in a hard voice. 'The job's too important.'

She loved arguing so Guy decided to be very calm.

'Yes, Miriam, I will,' he said.

'Go on then,' she said. 'Run away from everything.'

He tried to talk to her. 'Is there anything we can do about this, Miriam?' he asked.

'I've said what I want.'

◆

When Guy got back to his mother's house he found a letter from Anne:

What's happened? Write immediately, or phone. I want to be with you. Why don't you come to Mexico for a few days? Oh Guy, I'll miss you when you're away in Florida, but I'm so proud of you. Mum and Dad are, too. I know everything will be all right soon.

All my love,
Anne

After he read Anne's letter, Guy wrote to Mr Brillhart at the sports' club in Florida and said he could not take the job.

He spent the next day with his mother. That night someone rang him on the phone.

'Hallo,' a man's voice said. 'It's Charley.' He sounded drunk.

'Charley who?' Guy asked.

'Bruno! Charley Bruno!'

'Oh,' Guy said, 'Hello.'

'I've got your book, Guy,' Bruno said. 'Do you want me to send it to you?'

'Yes.'

9

'Oh, I know,' Bruno said. 'Come to Santa Fe and see me. Come now.'

'I can't,' Guy said.

'Okay. What about in Florida?' Bruno asked. 'I'll come and see you there. We'll have a great time.'

'No,' Guy said. 'That's all finished.'

'Why?' Bruno asked. Then his voice changed. 'Your wife, huh? I know, she wanted to go to Florida with you.'

This surprised Guy. How did Bruno know these things so quickly?

'You can still get a divorce, can't you, Guy?' Bruno asked. 'Guy? . . . Guy?'

'Look, I have to go,' Guy said.

'Guy, if you want me to do anything, you know, do anything, all you have to do is say.' Bruno's voice was thick and slow with whisky now.

Guy remembered Bruno's plan. He said angrily, 'I don't want anything from you. Understand?'

'Oh, Guy!' Bruno started to cry.

Guy put the phone down.

CHAPTER THREE

Guy was walking with Anne in Mexico City. In her long white dress and with her yellow hair she seemed to be made of gold.

'But did you have to refuse the job in Florida because of Miriam?' Anne asked.

'Yes. I hate her,' Guy said.

'Guy, you shouldn't hate people,' Anne said. 'You're talking like a child.'

He felt ashamed of what he said. Anne frightened him when she spoke like this. She seemed so far away from him. She was

10

calm and rich and clever and happy. Guy was not used to this. Sometimes, when he was unhappy, Guy thought he was the only problem in Anne's life.

They walked some more then Anne went back to the Ritz Hotel where she was staying with her parents. Guy went to his hotel. It was an ugly place, but Guy liked it.

The next morning Guy got a telegram from his mother:

Miriam lost her baby yesterday. She's very sad and wants to see you. Can you come home? Mama.

The first thing Guy did was to send a telegram to Mr Brillhart to ask if he could have the job again, then he rushed over to the Ritz to see Anne. They had a drink in the bar at the hotel.

'Are you going to Metcalf, Guy?' Anne asked.

'Not now, I'm too happy,' he told her.

'Do you think Miriam will follow you to Florida?'

Guy laughed. 'By this time next week,' he said, 'Miriam will be nothing to me.'

CHAPTER FOUR

Bruno sat in his mother's room at the Hotel La Fonda in Sante Fe and watched her put cream on her face.

'Charley,' she said, 'you won't do anything stupid when I'm in California, will you?'

'No, Ma,' Bruno said. He felt sick and his hands were shaking, but the idea was growing stronger and stronger: 'I must kill Miriam soon,' he thought, 'in the next few days or it'll be too late. Guy's in Mexico, Mother's going to California tomorrow, nobody in Metcalf knows me. If Miriam died now, Guy could get the Florida job back.'

'I need some money for tomorrow,' Bruno's mother said. 'I hope your father sends some soon.'

'That's all he's good for,' Bruno said. 'We don't need him.'

She put her hand against his cheek. 'My dear,' she said, 'I'll miss you.'

Bruno watched his mother walk into the bathroom. She had great legs; he really liked them.

He started thinking about the murder again. It would be perfect, a pure, clean **act**. He wanted to enjoy it. Perhaps Guy didn't want to kill his father, but that wasn't important now. Guy might do it when Miriam was dead.

Suddenly Bruno felt very unhappy. He could never tell his mother. ('Hey, Ma, I murdered this man's wife and then he killed Father. It was my idea, too. Aren't I clever? We're both free now!') No, he could never tell anyone, except Guy.

◆

Bruno tried to remember what day it was. Sunday, that was it. The time was 8.10 in the morning. He had plenty of time to get to Metcalf. He still felt drunk after last night and he wanted a clear head. He read the notes where he had written everything he knew about Miriam. He got out of bed slowly and walked very carefully around the room. There was one way to get better.

'I need a drink,' he said.

Outside the railway station Bruno went into a bar and bought a small bottle of whisky.

'Bruno!' a man called. It was Wilson and his friends. They were drunk, too.

'Hi, Wilson,' Bruno said. 'I can't talk. I have to catch a train.'

'Where are you going?' Wilson asked.

'Tulsa. I'm going to Tulsa. I've got some friends . . .'

Wilson wasn't listening. 'This is Joe,' he said. 'And this is . . .'

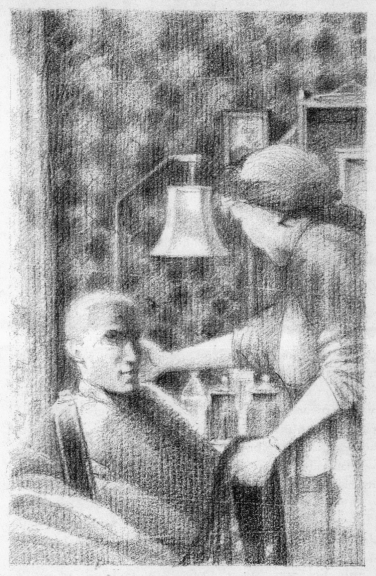

She put her hand against his cheek. 'My dear,' she said,
'I'll miss you.'

'I've got to go,' Bruno said. 'Bye!'

Bruno got on the train quickly. Did they know where he was going? No, they couldn't. The train started towards Metcalf and Bruno fell asleep before he could plan Miriam's murder.

CHAPTER FIVE

When he woke up Bruno felt better. His mind was clear, he felt happy and he was hungry. After a good dinner he read the notes about Miriam. What did she look like? She had red hair, was a little fat, and she was pregnant.

'The dirty little . . .' Bruno thought. He hated her. Guy would be happy without an animal like that in his life. Everything was so good. 'I have a friend, and my life has a real purpose,' Bruno thought. 'I'd do anything for Guy.'

When the train arrived at Metcalf station Bruno looked for Miriam's address in the telephone book. Miriam's family name was Joyce and she lived with her parents. There were seven people called Joyce in the book, one was a Mrs M. Joyce. Perhaps that was Miriam's mother, and she was called Miriam, too?

Bruno took a taxi to the address, 1253 Magnolia Street, and arrived at nine o'clock. It looked poor and ugly, the kind of place where Miriam would live. Bruno waited by a tree near the house. After a long time two men and a woman came out. The woman had red hair and a square, big body. One of the men had red hair, too. Her brother? They got in a car and drove away.

Bruno ran fast for a taxi. He never ran and it made him ill.

He found a taxi and got in. 'Go! Go!' he shouted at the driver. He could see the car in front of them. 'Right! Turn right now!'

'Where are you going?' the driver asked. 'Perhaps I know the place.'

'Shut your mouth and drive!' Bruno screamed.

The driver was annoyed and shook his head, but he followed the car. Eventually the car stopped in front of a big sign with lights. It said, LAKE METCALF'S LAND OF ENTERTAINMENT. There were music and lights and people laughing – an amusement park. Bruno smiled; this was perfect.

He followed the woman and her friends through the park. Was she really Miriam? She was quite fat, and her hair was red. Bruno noticed that she wore red socks with red shoes. Ugly! But this woman wasn't pregnant.

Then one of the men said, 'Miriam, do you want some ice-cream?'

'Oooh, yes,' she said.

It was her.

'You've got ten minutes to live and you're pushing ice-cream into your mouth,' Bruno thought. 'PIG!'

Miriam and her friends ran off laughing. They went on lots of different rides, they went round and round, and up and down. Miriam held her brother's hand, and then the other man's hand. She kissed him. Bruno hated her soft, fat face, and her stupid laugh. And what was she kissing these men for?

They all took a boat to an island in the middle of the Lake Metcalf, and Bruno followed in another boat. The island was dark and quiet, there were a lot of trees. People came here to kiss and make love. Why were the three of them here?

'Let's sit down,' one of the men said. 'I'll look for a place down here.' The other man went with him.

It was dark and Bruno saw Miriam's shadow alone against the water. Bruno moved quietly, and he was there next to her.

'Hello,' he whispered, 'Isn't your name Miriam?'

She turned. 'Yeah. Who're –?'

His hands closed round Miriam's throat and he pressed tighter

Miriam was silent and Bruno took his hands away. He ran down to his boat and went back over the water to the park.

and tighter. She couldn't scream. Bruno pushed her backwards and she fell over his leg to the ground. He pressed his hands into her throat more and more. Her skin was very hot. Her head turned from side to side, her lips opened and her teeth came forward. 'Sssssss,' she said. 'Ssssss.' Her throat was very fat. Bruno pressed her into the earth. She was very hot. It was like killing a hot little rat. He took his hands from her throat. Suddenly Miriam coughed, and Bruno jumped on her again and pressed and pressed her throat. He wanted her to die!

Miriam was silent and Bruno took his hands away. He ran down to his boat and went back over the water to the park.

'Help! Help!' Bruno heard the men shouting. 'My God, she's dead. Help!'

Bruno walked slowly out of the park. He needed a drink and went into a place that looked like a bar.

'Whisky,' he said.

'We don't sell drink here, son,' the man said.

'But I need a drink!' Bruno shouted.

'I don't have any whisky,' the man said. 'Coffee?'

Bruno left and ran to the station. He suddenly knew what he really wanted: a woman. He wanted a woman. He was very excited. He asked a taxi-driver where to go. The man wrote an address on one of his cards. Bruno ran off and the taxi-driver watched him until he turned a corner.

CHAPTER SIX

Guy sat back against his bed in the hotel and watched Anne turn over his drawings of their house. He kissed her hair and then her face.

'I want it to be a big house,' Anne said.

'Yes,' Guy said. He had the job in Florida again, which

would bring him a lot of money, and then there would be more valuable jobs. He was very happy.

'Are you hungry?' Anne asked. 'Let's order some food.'

As they ate, the phone rang.

'Guy?' It was his mother.

'Hello, Mama,' he said.

'Guy,' she said. 'It's about Miriam. She's dead, Guy. Murdered, last night . . .' She started to cry.

Guy put the phone down and told Anne about Miriam. He started to pack his suitcase while Anne ordered his plane ticket.

'Guy? Are you all right?' Anne asked.

Guy was staring at his drawings, but there were no houses on the paper, they were all drawings of Bruno's smiling face with his red, tired eyes.

◆

'What if Bruno did it?' Guy thought on the plane. He tried to remember every word they had said. 'Did I tell him to do it?'

At Metcalf the police asked him some questions and then Guy went home to his mother. He found a letter waiting for him. Inside was a card from a Metcalf taxi company and on the other side, some writing: NICE TOWN METCALF.

'That doesn't mean anything,' Guy told himself. 'It could be anyone. Lots of people come to Metcalf.'

At the **inquest** a lawyer asked Guy about Miriam.

'You wanted her dead, didn't you?' the lawyer said. 'You arranged her murder. You thought she wouldn't give you a divorce, and you didn't want her to go to Florida. Isn't that true?'

'Yes, but I didn't want her dead,' Guy said. He looked at Miriam's boyfriend, Owen Markham. He was a dark, good-looking man who looked at Guy with large brown eyes.

In the end the inquest decided that some unknown person had murdered Miriam.

The next day a telegram from Bruno arrived: ALL GOOD WISHES FROM THE GOLDEN WEST.

'It's from Anne's parents,' Guy told his mother. 'It's nothing – nothing.'

A few days later Guy went to Florida to start his new job. Every day he worked he felt good, he knew he was doing the right thing. The sports club would be a perfect building.

One evening in August he got a letter from Bruno:

I phoned your mother for your address, but she didn't give it to me. Look, Guy, don't worry. I'm going to be very careful. Write to me soon.

Your friend, Charley Bruno

Then Guy knew. Bruno did it, Bruno did it; he could not stop thinking those words, Bruno did it. His life was different now, his job, his mother, Anne, everything was different now.

When Guy spoke to his mother on the phone he said, 'Uh, do you remember that man who phoned you for my address? It was a friend, Phil Johnson. He works in Chicago, and he wanted to see me. Isn't that nice? Don't worry about it.'

CHAPTER SEVEN

'Charley, who're all these people?'

Bruno's mother looked at the stories about Miriam's murder and the photographs of Guy that Bruno had cut out of the newspapers.

'I met Guy Haines on a train,' Bruno said. He liked saying Guy's name, and he wanted to talk about the murder. 'Someone murdered his wife.'

'Who did it?' she asked.

'They don't know. It's a very difficult murder, a clever one, I think,' Bruno said. 'You know, Ma, Guy was the nicest man I ever met, but his wife was a –'

'Charley!' his mother said. 'You're in your grandmother's house and she doesn't like bad language.' She looked at the glass of whisky in his hand. 'Oh, Charley, you haven't had breakfast yet.'

'Whisky's good for me, Ma.'

'Don't drink too much,' she said. 'Come out later. You're in California and the sun is out. It's a beautiful day.'

But the whisky wasn't good for him. Every morning he had a pain in his chest and he couldn't breathe. When his mother left, Bruno thought about the murder. He felt so **powerful** – he took away life, like God! He wanted to tell everyone about the murder, about his one great act. Most people, ordinary, common people, never had one great thing in their lives.

'The newspapers,' he thought. 'I could tell them all about murder. I could teach them!'

Bruno really wanted to talk to Guy about the murder, but he did not dare to phone or write to him yet. But he had to talk to Guy soon, he wanted his father dead quickly, and he wanted Guy to do it.

Bruno's grandmother walked into the room.

'Have breakfast with me, my dear,' she said. 'Then I want to go out. A film, perhaps, a good one with a murder in it, or an amusement park?'

'An amusement park,' Bruno said with a smile. 'I like them.'

When they got back to the house in the afternoon there was a letter for Bruno:

Dear Charles
I don't understand your letter. I don't know you very well so please don't phone or write to me or my mother again.

Guy Haines

Bruno felt the terrible pain in his chest that he got in the mornings, and then he started to cry.

CHAPTER EIGHT

A few months later, in December, Guy sat in his office in New York. He was not getting any offers of jobs and he felt that his guilt about Miriam's murder kept people away from him. A man needed to be pure inside to draw plans for a good building, and Guy felt dirty.

He was making drawings of the house for him and Anne to live in after their wedding when the telephone rang.

'Hello, Guy, it's Bruno.'

Guy said nothing and put the phone down, but it rang again.

'I want to see you, Guy,' Bruno said.

'No,' Guy said and put the phone down.

That night he and Anne came out of his flat and Bruno was standing there in the dark. Guy held Anne's hand and tried to keep calm.

'Hello, Guy,' Bruno said softly. He looked at Anne with great interest, as if he was surprised to see Guy with a woman.

'We must go, we must go,' Guy said and walked away quickly, with Anne's hand still in his.

'Oh Guy, I just want to . . .' Bruno said.

'Who was that?' Anne asked.

'A man I know. He wants a job,' Guy said. 'It's nothing.'

'What does Bruno want?' Guy thought. 'What does he want?' The question did not go away, and Guy could not stop thinking.

♦

'What does Bruno want?' Guy thought. The question did not go
away, and Guy could not stop thinking.

One morning in January Bruno appeared next to Guy in the street and said, 'Have a drink with me, Guy.'

'No.'

'Yes,' Bruno said. 'What're you frightened of?'

'Nothing,' Guy said. 'Do I seem frightened?' ('Get the police!' Guy thought. 'The police, now!' But he couldn't.)

'Then have a drink with me,' Bruno said.

Guy agreed to go to a bar.

'Why didn't you tell me about Anne?' Bruno asked. 'That woman I see you with. I know all about her.'

'This is our last meeting,' Guy said. 'I'm going to tell the police about you.'

'Why didn't you do that last year?' Bruno smiled. 'I'll tell them you paid me to kill Miriam, tell them you went to Mexico so I could do it alone. They'll believe me, Guy.'

Guy knew this was true. He said, 'I have to go.'

'Wait,' Bruno said. 'You're going to kill my father.'

Guy looked into Bruno's eyes. They were the eyes of a mad child. Guy felt helpless, he could do nothing.

'I'll go to the police if you don't kill him!' Bruno said, then he left the bar suddenly.

◆

Over the next two weeks Guy saw Bruno standing outside his office every evening when he left. Then the first letter came. It was a map of Bruno's house with a written plan for the murder. Guy threw it away, but the letters came every two or three days. The twenty-first letter said: 'Do you want me to tell Anne about your part in Miriam's murder? You must kill my father soon, before the middle of March.' Then Bruno sent a big gun. Everything seemed like part of a bad **play** or film.

Guy looked at his own gun. He had bought it when he was

fifteen, because it was small and beautiful and perfect. He held the gun gently, and he smiled and thought about when he was a boy.

Guy spent the next day with Anne in the country, and they went to look at their house.

'It'll be finished by March,' Guy said.

'That's good,' Anne said. 'There'll be two months before we get married to buy things for it.'

'Do you know what . . .?' Guy began to say, then he stopped and looked at Anne from the sides of his eyes. He wanted to tell her about Bruno's letters and the gun, but he couldn't. He didn't want any secrets from Anne, but here was the biggest secret of all. Suddenly Guy realized that his life was separating into two parts, a life with Anne – and a life with Bruno.

They went back to Anne's house and before dinner Guy took a walk in the garden. He saw the black shape of a man – it was Bruno! Guy hit him hard and they both fell to the ground, but Bruno was very strong, and his hands went towards Guy's throat. Guy wanted to kill him. He pushed Bruno into the grass, fighting hard.

Suddenly Bruno said, 'Guy, you knew it was me!'

'I'll kill you the next time I find you here!' Guy shouted.

'Oh, Guy! Kill me if you want to!' Bruno said laughing, 'but are you ready to kill my father?'

'I'm ready to call the police,' Guy said.

'And I'm ready to tell Anne about you and Miriam, and then to tell the police!' There was a red light in Bruno's eyes; he looked like a hungry animal. 'I'll write to Anne tonight, Guy, unless you tell me you're going to murder my father!' He turned and ran away.

Now Guy was frightened. He waited for Bruno's letter to Anne to arrive. He knew he couldn't stop it. What could he say to her about the murder? He did want Miriam dead, he didn't

'Oh, Guy! Kill me if you want to!' Bruno said laughing,
'but are you ready to kill my father?'

stop Bruno killing her. He was guilty, too, and his guilt was growing stronger.

A few days later Anne phoned Guy. Her voice was shaking and Guy knew what had happened.

'I've had a letter, Guy,' she said.

'Oh?' He tried to be calm. 'A letter?'

'There's no name on the letter, Guy,' she said. 'It says you knew about Miriam's murder.'

'I don't understand, Anne,' he said. 'I don't know . . .'

'Guy, I won't tell anyone,' Anne said. 'But what's happening?'

'Nothing's happening, Anne,' Guy said, and thought his voice sounded strange. 'Can I see you tonight? We'll talk about it.'

'No. I can't,' Anne said.

Guy felt he was losing her, and that Bruno was everywhere. Then Guy realized something more: he had started lying to Anne.

CHAPTER NINE

The next day at work Guy had a call from Douglas Frear of the Shaw Company. He had sent the company some drawings for a building, and he wanted them to give him a job.

'Mr Haines,' Mr Frear said, 'I've had a letter – there's no name on it – and it says that you knew about your wife's murder and that the police want to speak to you.' He waited for Guy to speak. 'Mr Haines, I wanted to tell you about the letter. Are the police still asking questions?'

'No, Mr Frear, and I don't know who sent the letter,' Guy said. 'I don't know what it means.' Then he asked, 'Mr Frear, about the job . . .?'

'I'm sorry, Mr Haines, we gave that to another architect,' Mr Frear said quickly.

Guy went out for a drink. He was very worried. 'If I murder Bruno's father,' he thought, 'all of this will stop. No! I mustn't think that. But what can I do? What's the way out of this?' Guy drank some more and then went home. He slept heavily.

Early in the morning Guy woke up and felt someone in the room. He saw the orange end of a cigarette burning in the dark. He knew who it was and what he wanted.

'Bruno?' Guy said.

'You're ready now, aren't you, Guy?' Bruno said softly.

'Yes,' Guy said, and immediately felt better.

'Mother and I are going away tomorrow,' Bruno said. 'Do it tomorrow night. I broke the back door, so you can get in easily. Here's a key, too.' Bruno gave Guy some gloves. 'You'll need these.' His voice shook, 'Oh, Guy, I'll never see you again.'

CHAPTER TEN

Guy took the train for Great Neck that night. He had the gloves and his own small gun in his pocket. Bruno's gun was too big. It was raining when Guy got off the train at Great Neck. There was the bus, like Bruno had said in all his letters. Guy remembered all of it. At Grant Street he got off the bus and started to walk. There was the tree and the street light, and there was the white wall of Bruno's house. Guy felt like an actor in a play he'd already done hundreds of times.

Guy walked fifteen steps along the white wall, then he put up his hands and jumped on to the top of the wall. He looked down and saw the wooden box. There were no lights on in the house. Guy jumped down on to the box, landed without a sound, and ran across the grass towards the back door. He went up the six white steps near the back of the house and opened the back door – he didn't need the key.

The kitchen was dark. Guy walked across it and then went towards the back stairs that the servants used. Bruno had told him not to use the house stairs because they all made a noise. But Guy had to be careful here, too. He missed step three, step four and step seven on the back stairs because they made a noise.

Outside the door to one of the servants' bedrooms the floor made a noise, and at the same time Guy heard a clock – it was midnight. He stopped. The servant was on the other side of the door. The noise of the clock went on and on – could the servant hear? Now he remembered, Bruno had said, '. . . between eleven and midnight.' Was this why?

Guy felt very hot. Slowly, he opened the door into the part of the house where the family lived.

'I've been here before,' Guy thought. 'I've done all this before. I know everything about this house.' Again he felt like an actor in a play who did the same thing night after night. None of it was real.

Guy closed the stair-door quietly. And there, just there, very near, was another door – and behind that door was Guy's father. He walked quietly towards the door, and slowly opened it with his left hand. He held his gun in his right hand.

The bedroom was dark, but some light came through the window. It was only half open! Bruno said his father always had the window fully open.

'Because of the rain,' Guy thought. 'But how will I get out?'

Now Guy could see Bruno's father in his bed, sleeping quietly. There was the round, dark shape of his head.

'Ha-ha-ha-a!' came through the window.

Guy shook with fear. A woman was laughing somewhere outside.

'This man, this man is alive,' Guy thought. 'He could laugh,

Now Guy could see Bruno's father in his bed, sleeping quietly.
There was the round, dark shape of his head.

too, he could . . . No, don't think. Don't think. Do it now! Do it!'

He **fired** the gun. Nothing happened. It was all a dream, all a play, nothing was real! Guy fired again. Nothing . . . He breathed slowly and fired again. The room tore with a screaming sound. He fired a fourth time and the screaming sound came again, as if the world had burst.

'Kagh!' said the man in the bed, and his head moved.

Then Guy was running across the grass, but he didn't remember how he had got there. He ran like a man in a bad dream who runs and runs but cannot move.

'You!' A man's voice shouted behind him. It was the servant.

Guy stood in the shadow by the white wall.

'You!' the servant shouted again. Guy's hand shot out and hit him on the chin and the man fell to the ground.

Guy jumped over the wall, but it was very dark and he didn't know where he was. He tried to be calm, then he heard a police car very near him. The blue light moved over him for a few seconds.

'Where am I?' Guy thought. 'I can't remember . . . Where must I go?'

The blue light burned his eyes. He turned and ran away, then some trees caught him. The branches **scratched** his face and he pushed them away with his hands, but there were hundreds of them. He couldn't see, he couldn't think. He felt his own blood warm on his face and throat.

Finally, Guy got out of the trees and saw a road and the lights of a town. He walked slowly along the road. He still had his gun, but his gloves were torn to pieces. They were probably in the trees behind him. He was too tired to go back and look. He wanted to walk and never stop.

♦

The next day Guy looked at his face in the mirror. It was covered in scratches, and so were his hands. His body was heavy and tired. He thought he could never sleep enough in his life.

Guy read the papers. All the stories about the murder said the murderer was a big, tall man, nothing like himself. But it said the bullets were very small and Guy knew he had to throw away his gun. While he was reading, the doorbell rang.

'Hello, Guy. Guy! How did . . .?' It was Anne. 'Oh, Guy, what happened to your face? Your hands!'

'A fight. It was nothing,' he said. 'In a bar, a . . . Anne?'

Anne didn't say anything for a few seconds. 'But Guy, that letter, the fight you had in my garden that night, and now this . . . What's happening?'

He felt frightened, then he started to cry and couldn't stop. Anne put her hand on his shoulder, but she didn't try to hold him.

'If I tell her the **truth**,' Guy thought, 'she'll never touch me again.'

CHAPTER ELEVEN

Bruno sat and looked at Arthur Gerard, his father's private detective, and thought how ugly he was. Gerard had a fat pink face and little eyes, and he wore a dirty suit.

'I'll work on this murder for nothing, Charley,' Gerard said. 'I liked your father. I also think this is all very interesting.'

'I don't care what you think,' Bruno said.

'You hated your father, didn't you?' Gerard asked.

'He hated me.'

'Tell me about Thursday night again,' Gerard said.

'I left Mother about 2.45 in the morning, I went to get a hamburger, then I went to a bar, Clarke's,' Bruno said.

31

'Nobody saw you at Clarke's,' Gerard said.

'It was a different bar, then!' Bruno said.

'Okay, I want to know who you spoke to,' Gerard said. 'You see, I think it's strange that your father died on the night of the day you left. I think you spoke to someone, and they knew you were going away.'

'I said I don't care what you think,' Bruno said.

Gerard smiled. 'All right Charley. You can go now,' he said.

Bruno left Gerard's office angrily, but then he thought about Guy. Gerard was too stupid to find out about him.

'Guy and me,' Bruno thought, 'we're like gods.'

The next day Gerard came to see Bruno and his mother.

Bruno was sitting in the garden. 'Anything new?' he asked Gerard.

'We found these,' Gerard said, and showed Bruno some small pieces of the purple gloves. He looked across the grass. 'The murderer ran over there,' Gerard said, 'then he got caught in the branches of the trees on the other side of the wall. These pieces were there.'

'Really?' Bruno tried to sound interested.

'He knew where to go, too. The whole thing was planned, the box next to the wall, the broken back door . . .' Gerard didn't finish. 'I'll see your mother now.'

Bruno watched Gerard's fat body walk slowly across the grass. He tried not to think about Gerard, but the man seemed to be everywhere, and a few minutes later he followed Gerard into the house.

'Do you think Charley knew about the murder?' Bruno heard his mother ask.

'Yes, I think so, Elsie,' Gerard said. 'Don't you?'

'I'll certainly tell you everything he tells me, Arthur,' she said.

His own mother! What if she remembered all the stories about Guy from the paper? Suddenly Bruno felt alone. He wanted to sleep more than anything, but he needed more and more whisky for that, and he woke up earlier and earlier in the morning.

CHAPTER TWELVE

Guy had thrown away the big gun, the purple gloves, all the clothes he wore on that night, and his shoes, but he did not throw away his own little gun. He cleaned his flat again and again, especially at night because he only slept for two or three hours now. If he did not clean the flat, he tried to work. He had a job to plan a hospital, but how could he do that with so much guilt in him, with so much murder? He was not taking any money for the job.

How could he kiss his mother again? How could he talk to his friends? There was only Anne now. He still loved her, but his love for her made him two different people. The good man who loved Anne and built hospitals, and the bad man who murdered old men and helped to murder his wife.

The new house was ready, and one Sunday Guy and Anne and her parents went to see it.

'I hear there are lots of ducks and birds here. We could eat some,' Anne's father said. 'Are you good with a gun, Guy?'

They all looked round the house. It was only a month until the wedding now.

'We'll sit here every night as husband and wife,' Guy thought. 'How can I do that, when I know the things I've done?'

'Guy,' Anne said, 'Are you all right?'

'Yes,' he said, and laughed too loud.

'I think you're working too hard, you know,' Anne said.

Anne and her mother started to make dinner and her father made some drinks for all of them.

'What am I doing with these people?' Guy thought. 'They are so good, and I'm so bad. I'm not part of their family, but if I try hard to live with them, that other man inside me, the bad one, will go away. He must!'

After dinner Guy and Anne walked together in the garden. It was almost dark.

'I'm going to get a job with a company of architects in New York, Anne,' Guy said.

'But you have the hospital to do, Guy,' she said. 'That'll take you a year. Is it because you won't take any money for the hospital job?'

'Partly,' Guy said. 'But I just feel like it.'

'I know what the problem is,' Anne said.

'Do you, Anne?' Guy asked. 'Do you?' For a minute he wanted her to know everything.

'It's Miriam, isn't it?' Anne said. 'You've changed so much since she died.'

'No, no, I . . .'

'Do you want us to marry, Guy?' she asked.

He couldn't answer her. He almost didn't know how to speak to her honestly now.

Anne took his hand. 'I think,' she said. 'You need me a lot just now, and I need you a lot.'

Guy looked into her eyes and thought, 'If I can do this, if I can keep this all, the other man inside me will go away.'

CHAPTER THIRTEEN

On the day of his wedding Guy was waiting in the church with his friend, Bob Treacher, for Anne to arrive.

'Did you bring any whisky, Bob?' Guy asked. 'I need a drink.'

'Oh, yes,' Bob said. 'I forgot. Here you are.' He gave Guy the bottle with a smile.

Guy opened the bottle and put it on a table. After a few seconds he picked it up and threw it against the wall. Broken glass and whisky spread all over the floor. Guy stood with his back to Bob.

'I'm very sorry, Bob,' he said.

'It's all right, Guy,' he said. 'You're nervous.'

'No, I'm not nervous,' Guy thought. 'When are they going to stop this wedding? When are they all going to know about me? This is worse than the murder. I'm lying to Anne, but only she can save me.'

Guy could not stop the wedding. It was like the murder of Bruno's father. Guy felt he was an actor in a bad play, doing something he had done thousands of times before. At the party afterwards Guy suddenly saw Bruno's face smiling madly. Then it disappeared.

'Congratulations, Guy!' People were all shouting at the same time. 'Good luck, Guy and Anne.' The noise got louder and louder. 'Good luck! Good luck! GUY AND ANNE!'

'Good luck, Guy. I really want you and Anne to be happy, as happy as I am.' And there was that soft voice and that weak face with the mad red eyes in it and Bruno's hand was on Guy's shoulder and he was looking at Anne.

'Go away,' Guy whispered. 'You mustn't come here!'

'Are you a relation of Teddy Faulkner?' Bruno asked Anne. He shook her hand.

'He's my cousin,' Anne said.

'We play tennis sometimes,' Bruno said.

'Are you a friend of Guy's?' Anne asked.

Bruno laughed. 'Friend! I'm only his oldest friend in the world. We went to school together.' He put his arm round Guy's shoulder. 'Didn't we, Guy?'

35

'Friend! I'm only his oldest friend in the world. We went to school together.' Bruno put his arm round Guy's shoulder.

'You never told me about that man, Guy,' Anne said later.

'We didn't really go to school together, Anne,' Guy said quickly. 'I – I met him at the Parker Institute . . . it was last December.'

'Can't you see?' Guy thought as he looked at all the people in the room who were speaking to Bruno. 'Can't you see he's mad?'

CHAPTER FOURTEEN

Guy took a job with the company Horton, Horton and Keese, Architects. They gave him a big shop to build. It was easy to do, nothing special – anyone could do it.

He and Anne had their first party at the house soon after their wedding.

'Bruno's coming to the party,' Anne told Guy.

'Why?' Guy said. 'He isn't my friend.'

Bruno was drunk when he arrived. He looked at Anne all the time.

'I like your dress, Anne,' he said. Bruno always noticed women's clothes. 'Now, where will you go for your first holiday? Italy? You know, Anne, Guy and I always talked about travelling.'

Guy took Bruno to the corner of the room. 'Get out now,' he said. 'Or I'll kill you.'

'Is that a promise, Guy?' Bruno laughed. 'You know, Guy, I think Anne is very beautiful. I like it here.'

An hour later he fell behind the sofa, completely drunk, and went to sleep.

'He can stay the night,' Anne said.

'Where did you find him, Guy?' a man asked. 'They won't let him into our club anymore.'

A few days later Bruno sent flowers to Anne to say sorry for being so drunk at the party.

'Aren't they nice?' she said to Guy. 'I think Bruno's interesting.'

Horton, Horton, and Keese liked Guy's drawings for the shop. Guy hated them; this was the kind of ordinary work he didn't want to do. He wanted to leave the company, although they wanted him to do more work. But there was something much worse than this. A **normal** man could build a bad shop or a good hospital, but Guy wasn't normal. Sometimes he looked in a mirror and saw the other man who was inside him, the murderer, his secret brother.

The telephone rang and Guy's secretary picked it up.

'A man wants to speak to you, Mr Haines,' she said.

'Hello, Guy,' Bruno said. 'Come to lunch.'

Guy couldn't argue with Bruno in front of the secretary and he agreed to meet Bruno at a restaurant ten minutes later. Bruno had four expensive ties which he showed Guy.

'They're for you, Guy,' he said. 'Do you like them?' He was like a lover. 'Anne spoke to me on the phone this morning,' Bruno said. 'She told me you're both going on a trip. She's a great woman, Guy. You must be very happy.' For a moment Bruno wanted to hold Guy's hand, like a brother.

'Yes, I am,' Guy said. 'Very lucky.'

'What does Anne like doing, Guy?' Bruno asked. 'Does she like me?'

'You've never loved a woman, have you?' Guy said. 'You don't know what love is, do you?'

Bruno looked at the table. 'No,' he said.

'You give me ties,' Guy said, 'but you could give me to the police in the same way.'

'Oh, Guy!' Bruno started crying.

'I have to go!' Guy said. He jumped up and ran out of the restaurant.

'Why do people do this to me?' Bruno thought. 'Why? Why?'

◆

'How do you know Guy Haines's wife?' Gerard asked Bruno. He had all Bruno's bills, and he had seen the one for the flowers Bruno sent to Anne.

'I'm a friend of her husband,' Bruno said. 'Mother and I were thinking of building a house. He's an architect.'

'Why did you send Mrs Haines flowers?' Gerard asked. 'You must know them very well.'

'No. I went to a party there and I had a good time.'

'Let's talk about all these men you know,' Gerard said. 'Matt Levine, Mark Lev, you saw a lot of them before the murder.'

'Yeah, and Mark killed his own father, too,' Bruno said.

'Ernie Schroeder?' Gerard asked. 'Charley, please!'

Bruno tried to think of something to say.

CHAPTER FIFTEEN

Guy went on a sailing holiday with Anne on her boat, the *India*. They were away from home for three weeks. Guy was happy and calm. He looked at the clear sky and the blue sea, and the sea made him think of the bridge he wanted to build, a long white bridge like a pair of wings. He wanted to be a great architect. Guy saw Anne looking at him with love in her eyes, and he felt all the bad times were gone.

A few days later the phone rang at his home.

'Hello, Mr Haines,' a man said, 'this is Arthur Gerard. I'm a detective. Could I come to talk to you, at your house, please? Now.'

Guy had to say yes, and Gerard came over quickly. 'Do you know Charles Bruno, Mr Haines?' he asked.

'Yes, I know him.'

Gerard said, 'His father was murdered in March . . .'

'I didn't know that!' Anne said, and looked at Guy in surprise.

'Neither did I,' Guy said quickly. 'Murdered?'

'When and where did you meet Charles Bruno, Mr Haines?' Gerard asked.

'At – at the Parker Institute last December,' Guy said. He only said it because he had told Anne that at the wedding when she asked him about Bruno. Why hadn't he and Bruno planned a story?

'When did you see Mr Bruno again?' Gerard asked.

'At my wedding in June,' Guy said.

'And he came to a party in July, didn't he, Mrs Haines?' Gerard asked Anne.

'Yes,' she answered.

'Do you like him?' Gerard asked, smiling.

Anne looked at his smile; she didn't like it. 'Well enough,' she said finally.

Gerard asked them a few more questions and then he left.

'Does Gerard think Bruno murdered his father?' Anne asked Guy later.

'He probably thinks it's one of Bruno's friends,' Guy said. ('But it was me, Anne, it was me,' he thought.)

'You never know what people are really doing, do you?' Anne said, shaking her head in surprise.

Later in the day Bruno came to the house.

'You're drunk,' Guy said. 'Get out.'

'Perhaps we should get a taxi for you,' Anne said.

Bruno fell against Guy. He was saying the same thing again and again: 'I'll tell her – I'll tell her – I'll . . .'

'What?' Anne asked Guy. 'What's he saying?'

'Nothing,' Guy said. 'I'll put him to bed.'

Guy pulled Bruno out of the room and took him to a

40

bedroom. Bruno slept for several hours, and when he woke up Guy was with him.

'Bruno, listen to me, did you tell Gerard we met in December? At the Parker Institute?' Guy asked.

'Yeah, I said that,' Bruno said. 'Can I have a drink? Look, Gerard thinks this friend of mine, Matt Levine, murdered my father. He's already killed two or three men.'

'I won't let another man take the blame for the murder,' Guy said.

'He won't get the blame,' Bruno said. 'Gerard won't find anything about Matt Levine, or us. There's no **proof**.'

'Will you go now?'

'No,' Bruno said quietly. 'I want to be with you and Anne.'

And Guy knew that he hated Bruno, but liked him at the same time.

'You know, Guy, I like you, but you're in more trouble than me,' Bruno said. 'Our servant saw you that night, Anne saw those scratches on your face, and there's the gun, the gloves . . . the police could ask you some very difficult questions. But what have they got about me and Miriam, Guy? Tell me, Guy, what have they got?'

♦

Guy and Anne were on the *India*. The sky was grey and the air was hot. Guy held his little gun in his pocket.

'Why is Bruno so interested in you?' Anne asked Guy.

'He's got nothing to do,' Guy said. His hand tightened round the gun.

'And you met him at the Institute?' she asked.

'Yes.' Guy looked into the water. 'Why is she asking all these questions?' he thought. 'She knows something is wrong. She knows I'm lying, but she doesn't know about what.'

Guy heard Anne walk away. He quickly took his gun out of his pocket and dropped it into the sea.

41

*Guy heard Anne walk away. He quickly took his gun out of his
pocket and dropped it into the sea.*

'What was that?' Anne was standing behind him.

He could think of nothing to say to her.

CHAPTER SIXTEEN

'Ma, I don't feel good.' Bruno was in his mother's bedroom. He walked very slowly into her bathroom and got the bottle of whisky he had hidden there, but he dropped it on the floor. He couldn't control his hands.

'Charley?' his mother said and looked worried.

'I can't breathe, Ma!' He tore his clothes off. 'Oh God!'

'I'll get a doctor,' his mother said.

'No! They'll take me away!' He screamed, 'Look at my hands, Ma!' His middle fingers were bent tightly inside his hand. He couldn't stop it. He couldn't move them. 'Look, Ma!'

'Charley!' his mother shouted.

Bruno fell to the floor. He couldn't speak normally, 'Dome . . . Massom tehmeh . . . Ummm, Massom – Aaaagh!'

Then a doctor came and gave Bruno some medicine and he went to sleep.

'The drink is killing him,' the doctor told Bruno's mother. 'He must stop.'

Bruno woke up later and saw Gerard standing near the bed.

'I'm sorry to wake you,' Gerard said with his stupid smile, 'but I found something. Remember this?' He threw Guy's book on to the bed.

'I remember,' Bruno said.

'I got this book at the Hotel La Fonda. It's Haines's book. You met him eighteen months ago on the train to Santa Fe, didn't you?' Gerard said.

'No,' Bruno said. 'I found the book on the train, that's all. I wanted to send it to Guy but I lost it. I met him in December.'

'So you made calls to Metcalf eighteen months ago and you didn't even know Mr Haines?' Gerard asked. 'I found the phone bills.'

'Yeah, I phoned about the book!' Bruno said angrily.

'And you called before the murder, but you didn't call after,' Gerard said. 'Why not?'

'I don't know!' Bruno shouted. 'I'm tired of murder!'

'Oh, I believe that,' Gerard said. 'I believe that.'

A few moments later Guy had a phone call from Bruno in his office.

'Gerard knows about the book and the phone calls I made to Metcalf,' Bruno said very quietly, as if someone was listening. 'But I told him the calls were about the book and we met in December. All right?'

'All right,' Guy said and put the phone down. Gerard was coming closer and closer, but he couldn't stop it. He looked at the letter lying next to the phone. It was from his friend, Bob Treacher, in Canada:

I have an important job in Alberta. I want you to build a bridge for me as soon as possible. Write now.

Bob

♦

'Nobody knows who murdered Guy Haines's first wife, Miriam,' Gerard said to Bruno in his office.

'I know,' Bruno said.

'Did you talk to Guy about Miriam? You're interested in murder,' Gerard said.

'I didn't talk to him about it,' Bruno said.

'Do you think he planned it?' Gerard asked.

'No, I don't!' Bruno said angrily. 'You obviously don't know the type of man Guy Haines is. He's a great architect.'

'You obviously don't know the type of man Guy Haines is. He's a great architect.'

Gerard suddenly called out, 'Come in, please, Mr Haines.' He saw Bruno jump with surprise as Guy walked into the room.

'Did you and Charles ever talk about your wife's murder, Mr Haines?' Gerard asked.

'No,' Guy said.

'Did he ever tell you he wanted to murder his father?' Gerard asked. He had that slow, stupid smile on his face.

'No,' Guy said.

Gerard held up Guy's book. 'Charles found this on the train, but you didn't meet on the train, did you?'

'No,' Guy said.

'The waiter who brought dinner to the two of you in Charles's room on the train says you did, Mr Haines,' Gerard said, looking into Guy's eyes all the time.

Guy felt hot with shame. He couldn't speak.

'So what?' Bruno said angrily.

'So why are you both lying?' Gerard asked. 'Your wife was murdered, Mr Haines, a few days after you two met. And your father was murdered a few months later, Charles. Did you plan something?'

'We planned nothing,' Guy said.

'Did Charles tell you he wanted his father dead, Mr Haines? Perhaps you were frightened to tell me about it?' Gerard asked.

'No,' Guy said. He felt himself going deeper and deeper into his own lies. And when would Gerard find out the truth? Did he know it already?

Bruno and Guy left the office together.

'You know,' Bruno said. 'He's looking for other people. Gerard doesn't think we did it. We had no **reason** to do it, did we?'

♦

Gerard went to see Anne at home late one autumn afternoon.

'I think,' he said, 'that Charles Bruno told your husband about this plan to murder his father, and your husband didn't want to talk about it. Then, if your husband knew Miriam might die, too, they had a kind of secret, didn't they?'

'Guy couldn't do a thing like that,' Anne said.

'Do you think they met in March when Charles's father died, and you don't know about it?' Gerard asked.

'It's possible,' Anne said, but she didn't know why she said it. 'When was that fight?' she thought. 'February, March? And was it with Bruno? That was it. Guy tried to stop Bruno killing his father.'

'How was your husband in March, Mrs Haines?' Gerard asked.

'He was nervous,' she said. 'It was a difficult time. His work . . .' She stopped speaking.

Gerard looked at her, then he smiled and said, 'Call me if you think of anything you know, Mrs Haines,' and left quietly.

A few minutes later Anne saw Gerard outside the house, sitting in his car and writing notes.

'Why did I say that about March? Is he writing about that?' she thought.

'Gerard was here,' Anne said that night as soon as Guy came home. 'He wanted to know about March, if you knew Bruno had planned his father's murder for that month.'

Guy poured a glass of whisky, then he heard himself saying, 'Look, Anne, Bruno told me on the train that he wanted his father dead. I'm not going to say anything because the police can use that to hang an innocent men.'

Anne said gently, 'Yes, what you're doing is right.' And she smiled. 'It's terrible, isn't it, murder?'

Guy hated his lies. He felt empty inside. He thought he was worse than Bruno, who was honestly bad. Even if he was never caught, he couldn't live with Anne like this.

CHAPTER SEVENTEEN

Gerard smiled happily at Chief of Police Phil Dowland, and said, 'Can't you guess?'

'About Samuel Bruno's murder?' Dowland asked. 'You think his son, Charles, did it, don't you?' He didn't like Gerard because he was a private detective and he didn't work by police rules.

'No.' Gerard's smile grew wider. 'But I think he did another murder. Do you know Guy Haines?'

'Yes,' Dowland said. 'His wife was murdered last June.'

'Guy Haines and Charles Bruno met on a train to Santa Fe ten days before Miriam Haines died,' Gerard said.

'You think Bruno killed her?' Dowland asked. 'You've got no proof.'

'Yes, I have,' Gerard said happily. 'I've spoken to a friend of Bruno's, Edward Wilson, who saw him going to the railway station in Santa Fe on the day of Miriam's murder, a taxi-driver in Metcalf who drove Bruno to the amusement park the very night Miriam Haines died, and a man he tried to buy whisky from, near the amusement park – and another taxi driver who saw him, too. And I've got bills of phone calls Bruno made to Metcalf.'

'But why did Bruno murder this woman?' Dowland said, laughing. 'Because he met her husband on a train?'

'No,' Gerard said. 'You don't see, do you? It was a plan, Bruno wanted Guy to kill his father, and he did . . .'

'Guy Haines!' Dowland shouted. 'Oh, this is . . .'

'Yes, Guy Haines,' Gerard said. 'He didn't want to, but he had to after Bruno murdered his wife. Guy was frightened. It was all Bruno's idea, the perfect crime. There was no reason for

Guy and Bruno to murder these two people. They thought the police could never find them.'

'What happens now?' Dowland asked.

'I'm going on holiday,' Gerard said. 'I want to check some more details about Guy Haines. I can wait a few weeks.'

CHAPTER EIGHTEEN

Guy was living in Canada and building his bridge. He came home one weekend and saw a mess in the house only one person could make.

'Bruno was here,' he said.

'Yes,' Anne said.

'You know he's mad, don't you?' Guy said. Anne didn't answer and Guy looked at her carefully.

Anne thought, 'I know he's the one who wrote that letter to me in March, and the one you had a fight with. I know there's something . . .'

Then she said, 'Guy, I'm going to have a baby. Are you pleased?'

'A baby!' Guy said, and he laughed with happiness.

♦

The next day Bob Treacher came from Canada to stay with Guy and Anne. It was a sunny day, and the police had called to say that they had no more questions for Guy and Bruno about his father's murder. Anne was pregnant, he had a good job, he felt his life was changing and all the bad things were in the past.

The phone rang and Anne answered. 'Oh, hello,' she said. 'Yes, come with us. We'll meet you by the boat.' She said to Guy, 'That was Bruno, he's coming with us on the *India* today.'

49

And suddenly Guy felt everything seemed black again. It always came back.

They stopped for a friend of Anne's, Helen Heyburn, on the way to the boat, and Bruno was waiting for them when they arrived.

Bruno was very excited. 'Come on, Guy,' he shouted. 'This is a great day! We've won!'

'Won what?' Anne asked and Guy went cold inside. He looked at Bruno.

'Have a drink,' said Bruno, offering Anne his bottle of whisky.

'No, thank you,' she said.

'Come on, everybody!' Bruno shouted. 'Let's go!'

The boat moved quickly over the grey sea, and the wind was quite strong. Bruno ran about the boat.

'Sit down,' Bob said.

'Who are you?' Bruno asked drunkenly. 'A friend of Guy's?'

'Yes,' Bob said politely.

'I've known Guy all his life!' Bruno shouted. 'Have you?'

Guy saw Anne look at him with surprise. Every time with Bruno something bad happened.

'When will he say it?' Guy thought. 'The truth? He could say anything, do anything. For the rest of my life . . .'

'Come on, let's sing!' Bruno said. 'Guy, sing with me!'

'Oh, sit down,' Helen said to Bruno.

'Yes, sit down,' Guy said. 'And keep quiet!'

Bruno started to cry. They didn't want him. He tried to walk away from all of them, even Guy. Suddenly a large **wave** came up and hit the boat hard. The wave covered Bruno and with a scream he fell into the sea.

'Bruno!' Guy shouted. He jumped into the sea. It was very cold and the waves seemed to be as high as mountains. He saw Bruno's head very far away.

'Guy!' Bruno called once – a dying man.

Guy swam towards the place where he had seen Bruno, then

Suddenly a large wave came up and hit the boat hard. The wave covered Bruno and with a scream he fell into the sea.

he dived down into the cold grey water. The sea turned him round and round and round. There was nothing, Guy could see nothing. He was the loneliest man in the world. Where was his friend, his brother?

<h2 style="text-align:center">CHAPTER NINETEEN</h2>

Early one morning Guy got out of bed. He was very lonely without Bruno. He carried all the guilt inside himself now. He picked up some pieces of paper and started to write about everything, the train, Miriam, how he murdered Bruno's father. He left it for Anne to read.

'Anne is good,' Guy thought. 'The rest of us, Bruno, me, his father, Miriam, Gerard, all of us are bad.' Then he thought of Miriam's boyfriend, Owen Markham. He had loved Miriam, he was the father of her child. Guy remembered Owen at the inquest, where he seemed calm and gentle. Suddenly, Guy needed to talk to Owen. It was important, and after writing to Anne, it was the next thing he had to do.

◆

He took a plane for Houston, Texas, where Owen Markham now lived. Gerard had come back from holiday after Bruno died and Guy thought Gerard might follow him to Houston. He looked carefully at the other passengers on the plane, but Gerard was not there.

After asking some questions in different places in Houston, Guy found Owen in a bar.

'I need to talk to you,' Guy said. 'I've got a room at the Rice Hotel. Please.'

Owen looked at Guy with his calm brown eyes for a long time, then he said, 'All right.'

In the hotel room they drank whisky. 'Like the first time with Bruno,' Guy thought.

'I know the man who killed Miriam,' Guy said. 'I didn't stop him. I'm sorry, I know you loved Miriam.'

'No, I didn't,' Owen said, and drank some whisky. He spoke slowly. 'And I didn't want that child. She did that to make me marry her.'

It was all wrong, Owen didn't care. But Guy had to continue.

'You must listen to me,' Guy said. 'You must understand. This man, Miriam's murderer — his name was Bruno — he made me do a murder, too. His father. You see, we met on a train and Bruno said we should do the murders and the police would never catch us. He hated his father, Owen, it was frightening. I said I had some problems with Miriam but I wanted to divorce her. I said no to her murder, but then he killed Miriam, and I only knew after he had done it. You understand, I said no. But after her murder, Bruno phoned me again and again and wrote letters, telling me to murder his father. I was frightened he would tell my girlfriend that I knew about Miriam's murder. And I was tired of it all, so tired, so I said yes, and I agreed to kill his father. I only wanted Bruno to go away, that's all. I had to do it. Owen, I'm guilty, too. Do you hate me?'

'Hate you for what?' Owen asked stupidly. 'I don't know you. Who did you murder?'

Guy felt very tired. 'You have to go,' he said to Owen. 'You don't understand.'

Owen was very drunk and he didn't move.

'I'll call a taxi for you,' Guy said.

But where was the phone? Guy looked on the floor and saw it under the bed. The phone was lying near his chair so that someone could listen to everything he was saying. He picked it up.

'Hello?' he said.

Guy looked on the floor and saw the phone under the bed. It
was lying near his chair so that someone could listen to
everything he was saying.

'Hello, Mr Haines,' Gerard's voice said. 'I heard what you said to Mr Markham. May I come in?'

Guy opened the door and looked at Gerard's big smile. Guy tried to speak, but he said something completely different from what he wanted. He said, 'Take me.'

EXERCISES

Vocabulary Work

Look back at the 'Dictionary Words' in this book. Make sure that you know the meaning of each word.

1 What is the opposite of these four words?

   divorce   truth   powerful   normal

2 You can use six of the Dictionary Words in this book as either NOUNS or as VERBS: divorce, act, play, scratch, reason, wave.
   Sometimes they have different meanings when they are NOUNS from when they are VERBS. Write sentences to show the meaning of the six words clearly:

   a when they are NOUNS

   b when they are VERBS.

3 Match a word in group A with a word in group B:

   A: inquest   pregnant   architect   gun   proof

   B: plans   dead   innocent   baby   bullet

Comprehension

A

Chapters 1–5

1 How does Guy meet Charley Bruno?

2 Why does Bruno want to murder his father?

3 Why does Miriam want to go to Florida with Guy?

4 How does Bruno get to 1235 Magnolia Street from the railway station?

5 Where does Bruno kill Miriam?

Chapters 6–10

6   What is Guy doing when his mother phones to say that Miriam is dead?

7   Guy often says that he's going to call the police. Why doesn't he?

8   Which gun does Guy take to Great Neck? Why?

9   Why does Guy use the servants' stairs in Bruno's house?

10 How many times does Guy fire the gun? Why?

Chapters 11–15

11 How does Gerard know the murderer ran across the grass and jumped over the wall?

12 Why does Guy clean his flat again and again?

13 Why does Bruno come to Guy and Anne's wedding?

14 Does Gerard believe Guy and Bruno met in December? Why?

15 Guy hates and likes Bruno at the same time. What does he like about him?

Chapters 16–19

16 Why is Gerard interested in the phone calls Bruno made to Metcalf?

17 How many people go on the *India* the day Bruno dies?

18 Why does Guy call Bruno his 'friend, his brother'?

19 Is Owen Markham interested in what Guy tells him. Why?

20 In the final sentence what did Guy want to say that was 'completely different'?

B

1   At which part of the book is it too late for Guy to get out of Bruno's plan?

2   Why does Bruno hate Miriam and like Anne?

3   How does Guy's life slowly 'separate into two parts'?

4   Does Anne secretly know that Guy has done something wrong? How do you know?

5 Who says this? Who to? Where?

 a 'Men go to women like her like flies go to rubbish.'

 b 'I'll certainly tell you everything he tells me.'

 c 'You don't know what love is, do you?'

 d 'Do you think they met in March when Charles's father died, and you didn't know about it?'

Discussion

1 Bruno and Guy both murder someone. Do you think one murder was different from the other? Is murder always wrong?

2 Read Chapter 10 and then work with a friend: together draw a plan of Bruno's house and garden. Draw a line to show where Guy went. Look at other people's plans – are they the same as yours, or different?

Writing

1 Guy is in prison for murder and everyone knows the truth about the murders. Write a letter from Guy's mother to Bruno's mother. What will she say? Write about 150 words.

2 You are making a film of *Strangers on a Train*. Make a short plan for filming Miriam's murder on the island. Write some notes and make some drawings. A film is very different from a book and you might have to change some parts of the story.

Review

1 Is this a murder story, or a detective story, or is it about other things? What are they?

2 Do you want to read other books by Patricia Highsmith. Why?